This book belongs to:

Little Chimp's Big Day

by **Lisa Schroeder**   illustrated by **Lisa McCue**

STERLING

New York / London

To Sam and Grant: Make each day a BIG day!
And remember I love you always.
—L.S.

To Cameron and Cassidy: Full of chimpanzee spirit,
and destined for many adventures of their own.
—L.M.

STERLING and the distinctive Sterling logo are registered trademarks of
Sterling Publishing Co., Inc.

Library of Congress Cataloging-in-Publication Data

Schroeder, Lisa.
Little Chimp's big day / Lisa Schroeder ; illustrated by Lisa McCue.
p. cm.
Summary: While Little Chimp has a big day out by himself exploring,
playing, and discovering a big new world along with playmates, his mother watches nearby.
ISBN 978-1-4027-4967-4
[1. Stories in rhyme. 2. Chimpanzees--Fiction. 3. Animals--Infancy--
Fiction. 4. Mother and child--Fiction.] I. McCue, Lisa, ill. II. Title.
PZ8.3.S3775Li 2010
[E]--dc22
                                    2008015635
Lot#:
2 4 6 8 10 9 7 5 3 1
03/10
Published by Sterling Publishing Co., Inc.
387 Park Avenue South, New York, NY 10016
Text copyright © 2010 by Lisa Schroeder
Illustrations copyright © 2010 by Lisa McCue
Designed by Kate Moll
The original illustrations for this book were created using watercolor and acrylic paints.
Distributed in Canada by Sterling Publishing
c/o Canadian Manda Group, 165 Dufferin Street
Toronto, Ontario, Canada M6K 3H6
Distributed in the United Kingdom by GMC Distribution Services
Castle Place, 166 High Street, Lewes, East Sussex, England BN7 1XU
Distributed in Australia by Capricorn Link (Australia) Pty. Ltd.
P.O. Box 704, Windsor, NSW 2756, Australia

Printed in China

Sterling ISBN 978-1-4027-4967-4

For information about custom editions, special sales, premium and
corporate purchases, please contact Sterling Special Sales Department
at 800-805-5489 or specialsales@sterlingpublishing.com.

In the jungle, in a tree,
sits a little chimpanzee.

Mother said she'd be right back.
But now the branch snaps with a crack!

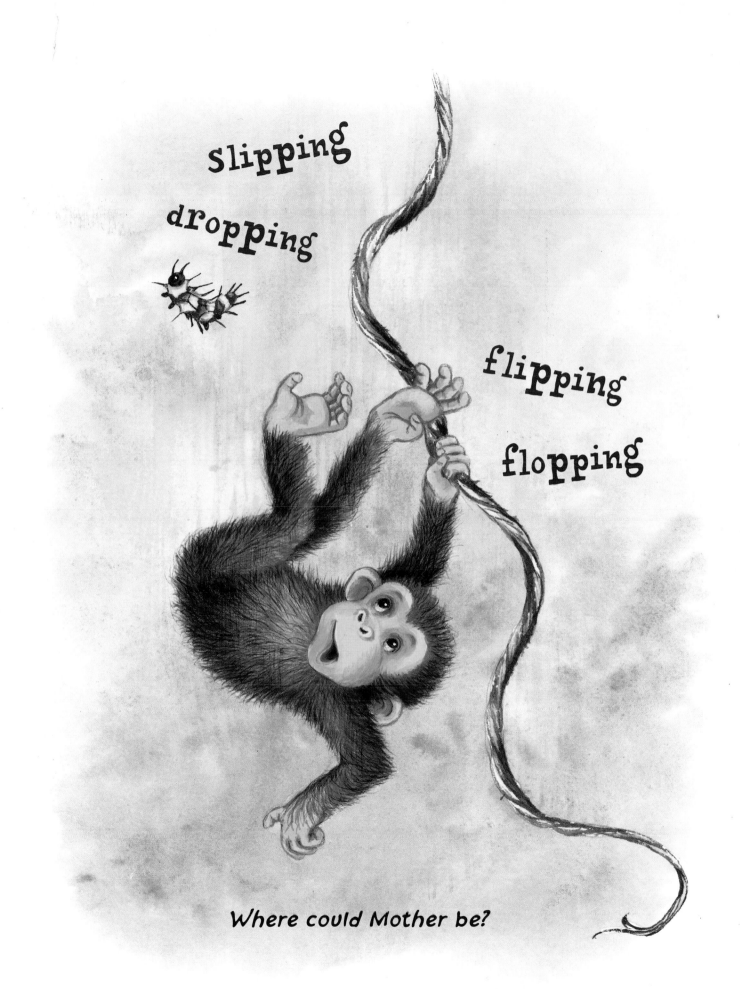

slipping

dropping

flipping

flopping

Where could Mother be?

Little Chimp lands with a thud
in a mucky patch of mud.

In the jungle, peek-a-boo,
two big eyes, peering through.

It groans and croaks and hops around.
What's this funny thing he's found?

bumping   chasing   jumping   raCing

Where could Mother be?

To the water's edge he goes,
stops and soaks his little toes.
In the jungle, by the stream,
things aren't always what they seem.

Chimp jumps on a rocky boat.
Wait a minute . . . rocks don't float!

grooving
gliding
moving
riding

Where could Mother be?

They stop and play beneath the falls.
Little Hippo hears Dad's calls.

In the jungle, friends must part,
but Chimp goes with a happy heart.

He is hungry. Time to munch
big bananas in a bunch.

seeking lurching
peeking perching

Where could Mother be?

Colors in the sky so bright.
Pretty parrots taking flight.
In the jungle, vine to vine,
through the rays of warm sunshine.

Up ahead, a jungle cat!
Little Chimp does not like that.

roaring

gripping

soaring

zipping

Oh, where could Mother be?

Little Chimp swings far and fast.
He yawns, then stops to rest at last.

In the jungle, in a tree,
sleeps a little chimpanzee.
He dreams about his busy day,
the fun he had along the way.

shaking
blinking
waking
thinking

Mother's finally HERE!

"Were you scared?" she asks her son.
He sticks his chest out. "I had fun."
She smiles and says, "My, how you've grown,
so big and brave, out there alone."

And then he whispers in her ear,
"But Mother, I'm so glad you're here."

Little Chimp crawls in her lap.
Suddenly, the branch goes

SNAP!

In the jungle, they climb fast. . .

. . . two chimps hugging,
safe at last.